WITHDRAWN

# THERE ARE MONSTERS EVERYWHERE

written and illustrated by Mercer Mayer

For Zebulon.
*You love all creatures, be they great*
*or small, be they tame or fearsome,*
*Zeb, you love them all.*

Dial Books for Young Readers

New York

DIAL BOOKS FOR YOUNG READERS • A division of Penguin
Young Readers Group • Published by The Penguin Group • Penguin
Group (USA) Inc., 345 Hudson Street, New York, NY 10014, U.S.A.
• Copyright © 2005 by Mercer Mayer • All rights reserved • Designed by
Diane Dubreuil • Text set in Bookman • Manufactured in China on acid-
free paper • Library of Congress Cataloging-in-Publication Data available
on request • ISBN 0-8037-0621-9 • 10 9 8 7 6 5

There were monsters everywhere in my house.

They would hide when my mom was around.

But when I was alone, the room would get very quiet. I just knew the monsters were going to jump out.

Dad said there weren't any monsters.
But he was wrong!

I knew there were monsters in the basement, but since I never had to go down there, they didn't bother me.

There were monsters outside by the
garbage cans too. I just knew it.

Dad had to watch me when I took out the trash, otherwise I might not ever return. He never seemed too worried, but I sure was.

There was a monster somewhere
in the bathroom.

I just knew he was there whenever I
shampooed my hair.

Sometimes I thought I heard him breathing.
But he vanished whenever I looked.

There were monsters hiding in my room. Mom
had to come with me to get my pajamas.

But they couldn't get me because I made a really good fort on the top of my bunk bed. Dad said monsters hate the top bunk because they're scared of ladders. I wondered if that was true.

I was really getting tired of being pushed around by a bunch of monsters.

Then I saw a sign for karate classes. All ages. *That means me*, I thought.

At dinner I told Mom and Dad that I needed karate class so the monsters wouldn't get me. They agreed that it was a good idea.

Karate was fun. I learned all sorts of
great-looking scary moves.

I even learned how to break a board with my bare hand. I was hoping a monster was watching when I did that.

The real test came one night after dinner. I took out the garbage and didn't ask Dad to watch me.

I could tell they were out there waiting. I gave a loud karate yell and kicked a garbage can. I think I made my point.

In the shower I practiced my karate punches on the shower curtain, just hoping a monster was standing too close.

Later I jumped into my room and took the most ferocious karate position I knew. Not one monster poked his head out. Ha!

I even slept on the bottom bunk.

The next day I went down to the basement.

I didn't want the monsters down there to think I was letting them off the hook.

I still go to karate class. I decided to get my black belt. I might even become a professional monster hunter when I grow up.

So, even though there are
monsters everywhere . . .

I don't care!